Tales of Mystery

Edgar Allan Poe

About this Book

For the Student

Listen to all of the story and do some activities on your Audio CD

Talk about the story

jug• When you see the orange dot you can check the word in the glossary

For the Teacher

HELBLING e-ZONE THE EDUCATIONAL PLATFORM A state-of-the-art interactive learning environment with 1000s of free online self-correcting activities for your chosen readers.

Go to our Readers Resource site for information on using readers and downloadable Resource Sheets, photocopiable Worksheets and Answer Keys. Plus free sample tracks from the story.

www.helblingreaders.com

For lots of great ideas on using Graded Readers consult Reading Matters, the Teacher's Guide to using Helbling Readers.

Level 5 Structures

Modal verb *would*	Non defining relative clauses
I'd love to ...	Present perfect continuous
Future continuous	*Used to / would*
Present perfect future	*Used to / used to doing*
Reported speech/ verbs/ questions	Second conditional
Past perfect	Expressing wishes and regrets
Defining relative clauses	

Structures from other levels are also included

Contents

HELBLING DIGITAL

FREE INTERACTIVE ONLINE TEACHING AND LEARNING MATERIALS

e·ZONE
THE EDUCATIONAL PLATFORM

HELBLING e-zone is an inspiring new state-of-the-art, easy-to-use interactive learning environment.

The online self-correcting activities include

- reading comprehension;
- listening comprehension;
- vocabulary;
- grammar;
- exam preparation.

1000s of free online interactive activities now available for HELBLING READERS and your other favourite Helbling Languages publications.

www. ONLINE ACTIVITIES
helbling-ezone.com

blog.helblingreaders.com

NEW

Love reading and readers and can't wait to get your class interested? Have a class library and reading programme but not sure how to take it a step further? The Helbling Readers BLOG is the place for you.

The **Helbling Readers BLOG** will provide you with ideas on setting up and running a Book Club and tips on reading lessons **every week**.

- Book Club
- Worksheets
- Lesson Plans

Subscribe to our **BLOG** and you will never miss out on our updates.

The Fall of the House of Usher

About the Author

Edgar Allan Poe was born on January 19th 1809 in Boston, Massachusetts, USA. His parents died when he was just two years old, and he was brought up• by John Allan, a Scottish businessman.

Poe was educated in Britain and the US. He was a good student and he attended the University of Virginia, and the famous West Point Military Academy. Poe spent two years in the army and in this period he completed his first two collections of poetry, published in 1827 and 1829.

Poe worked as a journalist and critic with several magazines and newspapers. He wrote many short stories including *The Murders in the Rue Morgue* (1841), *The Pit and the Pendulum* (1843) and *The Black Cat* (1843). These stories dealt with• dark, disturbing• themes and in America Poe was criticised for his 'Gothic•' writing style. In Europe, however, his work was popular and influential.

Poe suffered from illness and depression. The deaths of several close family members including his young wife Virginia affected him deeply. To alleviate• his depression Poe drank• heavily, but this caused health problems. His writing earned him little money, and he lived in poverty, accumulating debts. He died on October 7th 1849.

Poe's major contribution to world literature was the development of the short story as an art form.

Glossary

- **alleviate:** make less; make better
- **brought up:** raised; looked after when a child
- **dealt with:** talked about
- **disturbing:** that made people feel upset and uncomfortable
- **drank:** (here) drank alcohol
- **Gothic:** style of writing that concentrates on mysterious and desolate themes

About the Book

The three stories in this collection, *The Fall of the House of Usher, The Masque of the Red Death* and *The Oval Portrait* are examples of short stories in the 'Gothic' tradition. Gothic literature became popular in Britain in the late 18th century and it explores the dark side of human nature and experience: death, ghosts, alienation •, depression, madness • and desolate • settings. Poe brought Gothic literature to America. The atmosphere created by Poe in each of these stories is one of both physical and psychological fear and horror. Recurrent • themes in the stories are madness and death.

The Fall of the House of Usher was written in 1839. It is one of Poe's most popular horror stories and contains all the essential features • of a Gothic story: a frightening house, a desolate landscape, a mysterious illness, stormy weather and troubled • characters. The story, which tells of the demented • Roderick Usher and his strange twin sister, Lady Madeline, is now regarded as a classic short story masterpiece.

Poe creates a sense of claustrophobia in the story. The characters cannot move freely within the house. And the narrator cannot escape until the house physically collapses. Madeline and Roderick are twins and this stops them from developing as full individuals. Madeline is buried • while she is still alive and she finally kills her brother by falling on him and crushing him.

The story has inspired many other works including films, operas, plays, popular music, computer games and numerous works of fiction.

- **alienation:** when you feel isolated or that you are not part of society
- **buried:** when a dead body is placed in a grave
- **demented:** mad
- **desolate:** without life
- **features:** things that make something particular or special
- **madness:** state of being mad or crazy
- **recurrent:** that are repeated
- **troubled:** agitated; not at peace

Before Reading

1 **Look at these scenes from *The Fall of the House of Usher*. Discuss with a partner.**

a) Write at least 5 words or phrases to describe each scene.
b) What is the atmosphere like in each one?
c) What is happening in each scene?

2 **Working in groups of three or four, look at the pictures and your descriptions once more. Together write two or three sentences to describe what you think will happen in the story. Compare your summary with those of the other groups in the class.**

3 **You may find this story and the others in this book very frightening. Or perhaps nothing frightens you! Work with a partner. Describe your scariest experience, or something you heard or saw that made you feel afraid.**

4 Irrational fears are also called phobias. Can you match these phobias with their meanings?

a) ☐ arachnophobia	1	fear of closed spaces
b) ☐ claustrophobia	2	fear of storms
c) ☐ brontophobia	3	fear of dead things
d) ☐ agoraphobia	4	fear of spiders
e) ☐ necrophobia	5	fear of open spaces

5 What are you afraid of? Here are some of the things that make people feel afraid. How do they affect you? Rate them from 0 (not at all scary) to 5 (very scary).

a) ☐ bees and wasps
b) ☐ being on your own
c) ☐ exams
d) ☐ flying
e) ☐ going to the dentist
f) ☐ heights
g) ☐ lifts
h) ☐ the dark

6 Work with a partner and write sentences comparing how you both feel about the things above.

7 Listen to the opening of the story. Which of the sentences below best describes how the narrator feels? Tick (✓).

a) ☐ The narrator is looking forward to going to the House of Usher.
b) ☐ The narrator is indifferent to going to the House of Usher.
c) ☐ The narrator feels uneasy and unhappy about going to the House of Usher.

1 Read these sentences from the story. They all describe sounds. Then listen and match the underlined words with the sounds.

a) ☐ The suits of armour, which rattled as I walked were things which I remembered from my childhood.
b) ☐ The tapestries swayed fitfully to and fro making rustling noises about my bed.
c) ☐ Shaking off my fear with a gasp, I sat up against my pillows.
d) ☐ He lifted up his mace, and cracked and ripped the door, and tore everything apart.
e) ☐ Exactly as I had imagined the dragon's unnatural shriek to be.
f) ☐ There was the breaking open of her coffin, the grating of the iron hinges of her prison.
g) ☐ Then, with a low moaning cry, she fell heavily onto her brother.
h) ☐ The whirlwind gave a fierce blast.

2 Meet the three characters of the story. Look at the illustrations. Describe them. Invent as much detail as you can.

The Narrator

Roderick Usher

Madeline Usher

3 Here are some words that appear in the story. Match them with the pictures.

a) armour b) coffin c) lute d) shield
e) tapestry f) tree trunk g) vault h) web

1 
2 
3 
4 
5 
6 
7 
8 

4 Use the words above to complete these sentences.

a) Spirits danced happily around a king to the music of a ....
b) A .... of shining brass hung on the wall.
c) Dark .... hung on the wall.
d) The branches of the dead .... had once been green with leaves.
e) We opened the lid of the .... and looked at the face of its occupant.
f) Minute fungi were hanging in a fine tangled .... from the edges of the roof.
g) Suits of .... stood in the corridors of the house and rattled as I walked past.
h) The .... was small and damp, and did not admit any light.

5 In the story you will read about someone who goes to visit an old friend. Imagine that you go to visit a friend who you haven't seen for a long time. Your friend has changed. Write a short paragraph about the changes.

5 For a whole dull, dark, and soundless autumn day, when the clouds were low in the sky, I had been riding alone through the dreary countryside. Eventually, as evening fell, I found myself within view of the melancholy House of Usher. When I saw the building, I felt a sense of gloom.

PLACES

Have you ever visited a place and suddenly felt happy or sad? Describe how you felt. Why did this place make you feel this way? Was it something to do with the weather, the appearance of the place, or the people who were there?

I looked at the scene before me – at the house and the simple landscape, at the bleak walls, at the vacant eye-like windows, at the rough grass, and at a few white trunks of decayed trees – with a sense of depression, like an opium addict awakening from his dream. I felt a sense of iciness and my heart felt cold and heavy. What was it that made me so nervous when I thought about the House of Usher? It was a mystery, and I could not fight against the dark thoughts that filled me.

Glossary

- **bleak:** empty, cold and depressing
- **decayed:** rotten; destroyed through age
- **dreary:** boring and dark; without life
- **dull:** not bright
- **gloom:** darkness and depression

I was forced to come to the unsatisfactory conclusion that some things are beyond our understanding. If the scene in front of me had been arranged in any different way it possibly would not have left me with such a sad impression. With this in mind, I rode my horse to the edge of a black lake that was close to the house and, trembling more than before, I looked down on the reflection of the grey grass, the ghastly• tree trunks, and the empty eye-like windows in the water.

Nevertheless, I was proposing to stay a few weeks in this gloomy house. Its owner, Roderick Usher, had been one of my childhood companions, but it had been many years since our last meeting. A letter from him had reached me, and it gave evidence that he was very disturbed. The writer spoke of physical illness, and of a disorder of the mind. He said I was his best and only friend, and he felt that the cheerfulness of my company would lessen• his malady•. I did not hesitate when I read this. I obeyed his request immediately.

RODERICK USHER

How does the narrator know Roderick Usher?
Why does Usher write to the narrator?
What does Usher ask the narrator to do?

Glossary

- **ghastly:** horrible and frightening
- **lessen:** make less
- **malady:** illness

Although, as boys, we had been quite close, I knew very little about my friend. He had always been very reserved. I was aware, however, that his family had displayed its talent over the years in many works of art. They had also performed repeated acts of charity, as well as showing passionate devotion to music. I learned too that, for the most part, the Usher family had never produced any continuing branch. And that the entire family was in a direct line of descent. Indeed this had always been the case with very little variation.

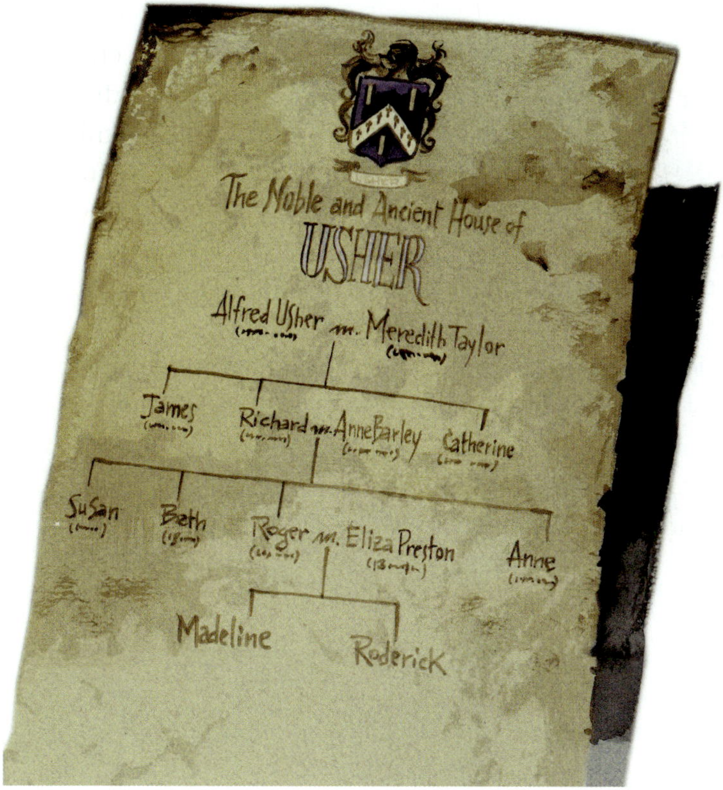

- **branch:** descendants; sons, daughters, grandchildren. etc.
- **direct line of descent:** there was always just one child who had children of their own
- **I was aware:** I knew
- **produced:** (here) had children
- **reserved:** quiet; shy; private

I began to think about how the character of the house perfectly matched the character of the people who lived in it, and I speculated on the possible influence that, over the centuries, the one might have exercised on the other. Indeed it was this lack of descendants, and the continual passing down from father to son of the family home along with the family name, which had eventually caused both to be identified with the title of the estate: the 'House of Usher'. In the minds of the peasantry who used it, this title seems to include both the family and the family mansion.

FAMILY

What do we know about the Usher family?
Tick the correct answers.

- ☐ Roderick has got a large extended family.
- ☐ Roderick's family are interested in the arts.
- ☐ Roderick's family inherited the house recently.
- ☐ The Usher family has always been small.

Now think of your own family.
How far can you trace your family tree?

Glossary

- **estate:** a family's house and land
- **exercised:** (here) had
- **lack:** absence
- **mansion:** large noble house
- **passing down:** giving from one generation to the next
- **peasantry:** country people
- **perfectly matched:** was exactly like
- **speculated:** guessed (about)

When I looked up again at the house itself, from its image in the water, a strange thought grew in my mind. It was a thought so ridiculous that I only say it to show the strength of the feelings that oppressed me. I had concentrated so much on my imagination that I really believed there was an atmosphere around the whole house and surrounding area that had no connection with the air of heaven. This atmosphere seemed to come from the decayed trees, the grey wall, and the silent lake like a pestilent and mysterious vapour.

Shaking off from my spirit what felt like a dream, I looked at the building in more detail. Its main feature seemed to be its excessive age. It was discoloured, and tiny fungi covered the whole exterior, hanging in a fine tangled web from the edges of the roof. There appeared to be some inconsistency between the apparently perfect state of the bricks, and the crumbling condition of the individual stones. Apart from this sign of extensive decay, the construction gave little sign of instability. Perhaps a careful observer might have discovered a barely perceptible crack extending from the roof of the building in front, and that zigzagged down the wall until it became lost in the waters of the lake.

6 Noticing these things, I rode over a short bridge to the house. A servant took my horse, and I entered the Gothic archway of the hall. A valet led me, in silence, through many dark winding corridors to his master's room. Much of what I saw on the way contributed to increase the feelings of which I have already spoken. The objects around me, the carvings on the ceilings, the dark tapestries on the walls, the black floors, and the suits of armour, which rattled as I walked, were all things which I remembered from my childhood.

- **barely perceptible:** that was difficult to see
- **crack:** break in a wall
- **crumbling:** breaking into small parts
- **inconsistency:** difference
- **pestilent:** that causes disease
- **ridiculous:** silly; absurd
- **tangled:** confused mass; mixed
- **valet:** male servant of a man
- **vapour:** air with tiny drops of liquid
- **winding:** with many turns; not straight

Still, I was surprised at the unfamiliar thoughts that these ordinary images were creating in me. On one of the staircases, I met the physician of the family. I thought he had a puzzled expression on his face. He seemed agitated and walked past me. The valet opened a door and accompanied me in to the presence of his master.

The room in which I found myself was very large and high. The windows were long and narrow, and at a vast distance from the black wooden floor, making them inaccessible from inside the room. Feeble rays of light filtered through the window panes, so that it was possible to see the more prominent objects; however, it was difficult to see the remoter corners of the room, or the ceiling. Dark tapestries hung on the walls. The furniture was old and tattered. Many books and musical instruments lay scattered about. I felt that I was breathing an atmosphere of sadness. An air of gloom pervaded everything.

WARNING SIGNS

Think about what the narrator has seen and thought so far. What signs are there to warn us that something is wrong in the House of Usher?

Glossary

- **feeble:** not strong; weak
- **inaccessible:** that cannot be reached
- **panes:** sheets of glass
- **pervaded:** filled
- **physician:** doctor
- **puzzled:** confused
- **scattered:** placed in an untidy way
- **tattered:** torn; in rags

When I entered, Usher rose from a sofa on which he had been lying, and greeted me warmly, but I thought he did so with exaggerated cordiality•. A glance• at his face, however, convinced me of his sincerity. We sat down and for some moments I looked at him with a feeling half of pity, half of awe•. No man had changed so much in such a brief period as Roderick Usher had! It was with difficulty that I recognised as my childhood friend the pale man in front of me. The features of his face had always been unique. He had the pale skin of a corpse•, eyes that were large and luminous, and lips that were thin and very pale, but that had a beautiful shape. His nose was delicate, but with broad nostrils•. He had a finely shaped chin, and hair that had a web-like softness. These features, together with a wide forehead, made up a face that was not easily forgotten. Now his features were exaggerated, and everything about him was so different that I doubted that I was speaking to my friend. The paleness of the skin, and the shiny look of his eyes shocked me most of all. The silky hair, too, had grown long and wild, and it floated around his face. I could not, even with effort, think of him as someone normal.

I was struck by my friend's incoherence•. But I soon discovered that this came from his attempts to overcome• his nervousness. I had been prepared for this both from his letter and from my memory of certain physical and emotional characteristics he had had when he was a boy. One minute he was lively and the next he was quiet. His voice changed often, from being trembling and indecisive to sounding like the voice of someone who is drunk• or drugged•.

Glossary

- **awe:** great admiration
- **cordiality:** friendliness
- **corpse:** dead body
- **drugged:** who has taken drugs
- **drunk:** who has drunk too much alcohol
- **glance:** quick look
- **incoherence:** when someone is not clear when speaking
- **nostrils:** the two holes in the nose
- **overcome:** defeat; win over

He spoke about the purpose• of my visit, of his earnest• desire to see me, and of the comfort he expected to have from my presence. He talked at some length about what he believed to be the nature of his malady. It was, he said, a sickness that was in his family, and one for which he had lost hope of finding a remedy•.

He immediately added that it was only a nervous complaint•, which would undoubtedly go away soon. It showed itself in various unnatural sensations. Some of these interested and bewildered• me although this may have been because of the way he described them. He suffered from an acuteness• of the senses. He could only eat the most simple food and he could only wear clothes of a certain texture. He found the smell of all flowers oppressive, the smallest quantity of light tortured his eyes, and only a few sounds, mostly those from stringed instruments•, did not fill him with horror.

Glossary

- **acuteness:** extreme sensitivity; sharpness
- **bewildered:** confused
- **complaint:** (here) illness
- **earnest:** sincere
- **purpose:** reason
- **remedy:** cure to make him better
- **stringed instruments:** instruments with strings (guitars, lutes, etc.)

ILLNESS

What are the outward signs of Usher's illness?
Is there anything strange about his symptoms?
What do you think is wrong with him?
Is his illness real or imaginary?
Write how his illness affects his senses.

He was a slave to an abnormal kind of terror. 'I shall die', he said, 'I *must* die because of this fear. Not for any other reason. I dread• the events of the future. I have no fear of danger, but I feel that the time will arrive sooner or later when I will have to give up• both my life and my reason• in my struggle with this terrible FEAR.'

Little by little and through occasional hints•, I learned another particular feature of his mental condition. He was obsessed by certain superstitious• ideas about the house in which he lived, and which he had never left for many years. Over a long period of time the building with its grey walls and towers, and the dim• lake into which they all looked, had gained• control over his spirit.

- **dim:** not bright; dark
- **dread:** (here) hate the thought of
- **gained:** got; won
- **give up:** (here) lose
- **hints:** suggestions; small indications
- **reason:** logic; mind
- **superstitious:** (here) not scientific

He admitted, with hesitation, that much of his sadness could be traced• to a more natural origin – to the severe and lengthy illness, indeed to the approaching death, of his much loved sister. His sister had been his only companion for many years and she was his last and only relative on earth. 'Her death', he said, with a bitterness• I can never forget, 'would leave me as the last of the ancient race of the Ushers.'

As he spoke, Lady Madeline (this was her name) passed slowly through a remote part of the room and disappeared without noticing me. I watched her with astonishment mixed with dread•, and yet I found it impossible to explain these feelings. My eyes followed her as if I were in a trance•. When eventually a door closed behind her, I turned instinctively to look at her brother. He had buried his face in his hands, and I could see that an unusual whiteness had spread across his emaciated• fingers and through them many tears trickled•.

Lady Madeline's disease had puzzled her doctors for a long time. Her unusual symptoms were apathy, a gradual wasting away• of her body, and frequent periods of falling into a deep sleep. Up to now she had coped• with her malady, and she had not stayed in her bed. But, on the evening of my arrival at the house, she gave in• to her illness (as her brother told me that night with great agitation). I knew that I would probably never see the lady alive again.

Glossary

- **bitterness:** sad and resentful feeling
- **coped:** (here) managed to live
- **dread:** (here) fear
- **emaciated:** very thin
- **gave in:** stopped fighting
- **traced:** (here) connected
- **trance:** hypnotic state
- **trickled:** moved slowly (of liquid)
- **wasting away:** becoming very thin

In the following days we did not mention her name again. During this period I was busy trying to lighten• my friend's mood•. We painted and read together, or I listened, as if in a dream, as he played his guitar. But as I grew closer to him I realised the futility of all my attempts to cheer• a mind that was full of darkness and gloom.

MOODS

What activities does the narrator involve Usher in to cheer him up?
What about you?
If you feel sad or upset, what helps you to feel better?
What do you do to change your mood?
When you are sad do you like to see friends or do you prefer to be on your own?

I shall always remember the many solemn hours I spent alone like this with the master of the House of Usher. Yet I would not be able to explain the occupations in which he involved me. The dull music he improvised• will ring• forever in my ears. His paintings thrilled• me and filled me with awe with their vivid• images yet I could only understand a small part of their meaning. If ever a person painted an idea that person was Roderick Usher.

Glossary

- **cheer:** make happy
- **improvised:** played without planning
- **lighten:** make light; lift
- **mood:** how you feel
- **ring:** sound
- **thrilled:** made happy and enthusiastic
- **vivid:** bright and intense

One of the ghostly pieces that my friend produced, which was less abstract than the rest, I can describe in words. A small picture showed the interior of a long, rectangular tunnel, with low smooth white walls. The picture conveyed the idea that this tunnel lay deep below the surface of the earth. There were no visible doors or openings, and no torch or other source• of artificial light could be seen, yet a flood• of intense rays filled the whole scene with inappropriate splendour.

I have already mentioned• the condition of the auditory• nerve that made all music intolerable to the sufferer, except for certain notes played on stringed instruments. He had to confine himself to narrow• limits on the guitar and this perhaps was the reason for his strange performances. However it does not explain the wild passion of the verbal improvisations he often used to accompany his guitar. I remember well the words of one of these rhapsodies•. Listening to him I had the impression that he was aware for the first time that he was going mad.

The verses, which were entitled 'The Haunted Palace', told of a wonderful palace full of jewels and fine things in which spirits danced happily around their king to the music of a lute•. The inhabitants of the palace sang songs in beautiful voices praising the wisdom• of their ruler. But then one day evil creatures entered the palace and killed the king. That was many years ago. Now travellers who are passing by and who look through the windows into the palace see ghosts dancing to a discordant• melody.

- **auditory:** hearing
- **discordant:** not in harmony
- **flood:** (here) large quantity
- **lute:** musical instrument like a guitar
- **mentioned:** talked about
- **narrow:** very small
- **rhapsodies:** compositions
- **source:** origin; where something starts
- **wisdom:** wise nature

I well remember that discussions of this ballad • led us to an opinion of Usher's that I mention not so much because of its novelty (for others have had the same idea) but because of the insistence with which he maintained it. This opinion, in its general form, was about the ability of inanimate • things or objects to begin to feel sensations. The idea was connected in his mind (as I have previously hinted •) with the grey stones of the home of his ancestors. The sensations arose, he imagined, from how these stones had been placed, one on top of the other, as well as from the fungi that spread over • them, and the decayed trees that stood around the building. And, he added, from the long period that the house and its reflection in the still waters of the lake had been left undisturbed. The evidence of these sensations could be seen, he said, in how the water and walls had gradually created an atmosphere of their own. The result of this was evident, he added, in that terrible influence which for centuries had moulded • the destinies of his family, and which made him what he was. Such opinions need no comment, and I will make none.

BELIEFS

What does Usher believe about the things around him and about the house in which he lives? Tick.

☐ He thinks the atmosphere of the house has had a good influence on his family.

☐ He thinks the atmosphere of the house has had a bad influence on his family.

Glossary

- **ballad:** poem or piece of music with a story
- **hinted:** suggested
- **inanimate:** not living
- **moulded:** shaped; created
- **spread over:** covered

The books we read, and which for years had occupied the mental existence of the invalid, were, as might be supposed, in strict keeping• with Usher's beliefs. We spent hours together studying works of the supernatural, demonism and the occult• by authors such as Gresset, Macchiavelli, Swedenborg, Holberg, D'Indaginé, De la Chambre, Tieck, and Campanella. One favourite volume• was an edition• about the Inquisition•, the Directorium Inquisitorum, by the monk Eymeric de Gironne, and there were passages• in Pomponius Mela, about the old African Satyrs and OEgipans, creatures that were half man and half goat, over which Usher would sit dreaming for hours. His main delight•, however, was found in the perusal• of an exceedingly rare and curious book about a forgotten church, the Vigiliae Mortuorum Secundum Chorum Ecclesiae Maguntinae, which contained songs for the dead.

- **delight:** happiness
- **edition:** book
- **Inquisition:** The Spanish Inquisition (period between 1478 and 1834 when the Catholic Church questioned and tortured people who were believed to be against the Catholic religion)
- **in strict keeping:** closely connected
- **occult:** supernatural
- **passages:** short parts of a book
- **perusal:** reading carefully; study
- **volume:** book

READING

Do you read in your free time?
What do you like to read?
How much time do you spend reading every week?
Where do you usually read?
Work with a partner and compare your reading habits.
What do Usher's reading habits tell us about him?

7 I could not help thinking of the probable influence that these books were having upon Usher, when, one evening, after informing me abruptly• that Lady Madeline was no more, he stated his intention of preserving• her corpse for a fortnight, before its final burial, in one of the numerous vaults• within the walls of the building. The reason for this unusual procedure• was one which I did not feel at liberty to dispute.

The brother had reached this decision, he told me, after considering the unusual nature of the malady of the deceased•, and after considering that her doctors might interfere and ask questions about her illness, and because the family's burial ground was in a remote and exposed• place. I will not deny• that when I thought of the sinister• appearance of the physician who I saw on the day of my arrival at the house, I had no desire to oppose what I regarded as just a harmless, and by no means unnatural, precaution.

Glossary

- **abruptly:** suddenly
- **deceased:** dead person
- **deny:** disagree
- **exposed:** open to danger or damage
- **preserving:** keeping
- **procedure:** way of acting
- **sinister:** evil and dangerous
- **vaults:** underground rooms

At Usher's request, I personally helped him in the arrangements• for the temporary entombment•. The body was placed in a coffin•, then we two alone carried it to its rest. The vault in which we placed the coffin had been closed for such a long time that our torches were half smothered• in its oppressive atmosphere and therefore we did not have an opportunity to investigate it. The vault was small and damp•, and did not admit any light. It lay at a great depth, immediately beneath my own bedroom. It had been used, apparently, in remote times, as a dungeon• and possibly as a torture chamber. It had then been used as a place for the deposit of gunpowder• or some other highly combustible• substance, since part of its floor and the whole interior of a long archway through which we had reached it, were carefully covered with copper. The door, of heavy iron, had also been similarly protected.

- **arrangements:** organization
- **coffin:** box for dead people
- **combustible:** that explodes
- **damp:** wet
- **dungeon:** underground prison
- **entombment:** burial
- **gunpowder:** explosive that was used in guns in the past
- **smothered:** covered; dead from no oxygen

We placed Lady Madeline upon trestles• inside the vault, and then moved aside the unscrewed• lid of the coffin, and looked upon the face of the occupant•. My attention was now drawn• to the striking• similarity between the brother and sister, and Usher, probably guessing my thoughts, murmured a few words from which I learned that he and Lady Madeline had been twins. Our stares• did not rest on the dead sister for long because we could not look at her without feeling disturbed. The disease which had caused Lady Madeline to die at this early age, had left, as was usual in all maladies that had trance-like symptoms, a faint blush• on her neck and face, and a lingering• smile on her lips. We replaced and screwed down the lid and, having locked the iron door, we made our way to the rooms in the upper part of the house.

Glossary

- **blush:** red colour on cheeks
- **drawn:** (here) brought
- **lingering:** that stays for a period
- **occupant:** the person inside the coffin (Lady Madeline)
- **stares:** long looks
- **striking:** (here) unusual; remarkable
- **trestles:** wooden supports
- **unscrewed:** not locked

THE BURIAL OF LADY MADELINE

When someone dies, what is the normal reaction of that person's family and friends?

How does Usher react when his sister dies?

What is unusual about the burial of Lady Madeline?

What do we find out about the 'malady' that killed her?

What is the special connection between Usher and Lady Madeline?

After a few days of bitter grief had passed, there was a noticeable change in my friend's mental disorder. His usual manner had vanished. His ordinary occupations were neglected or forgotten. He moved from room to room. The paleness of his face had assumed a more sickly colour, and the light in his eyes had gone completely. His usual tone of voice was heard no more and instead he spoke with a trembling voice as if he were in great fear. There were times when I thought that his agitated mind was trying to keep some oppressive secret and that he was struggling for the courage to reveal it.

SECRETS

Do you find it easy to keep a secret?
Was there ever a time when you could not keep a secret?
When is it right to tell a secret?
When is it wrong to tell a secret?
What do you think Usher's secret is?

At times I thought he was suffering from an inexplicable form of madness, because I saw him gazing vacantly for hours, as if listening to some imaginary sound. It was no wonder that his condition terrified me. I felt the wild influences of his fears creeping upon me, by slow yet certain degrees.

Glossary

- **assumed:** (here) taken on
- **bitter:** terrible
- **gazing:** looking
- **grief:** sadness (after someone dies)
- **neglected:** given little attention
- **sickly:** that seemed sick
- **vanished:** disappeared

8 It was after retiring• to bed late on the night of the seventh or eighth day after we had placed Lady Madeline inside the vault, that I experienced the full power of this fear. I was unable to sleep and the hours slowly passed. I struggled• to understand the reason for these nervous feelings that had taken control of me. I tried to convince myself that much of what I felt was due to the influence of the gloomy furniture in the room, of the dark and tattered tapestries which, because of the storm outside, swayed fitfully to and fro• making rustling• noises about my bed.

But my efforts were useless. I could not stop myself from trembling, and my heart felt deeply alarmed. Shaking off my fear with a gasp• and a struggle, I sat up against my pillows. I stared into the intense darkness of the room, and listened to certain indistinct sounds which came at intervals through the pauses in the storm. I was overpowered• by an intense and unbearable• feeling of horror that I could not explain. I got dressed quickly (for I felt that I would sleep no more during that night), and tried to awake• myself from the condition into which I had fallen by walking rapidly around my room.

I had done this a few times when the sound of a light step on an adjoining• staircase caught my attention. I recognized it as Usher's footstep. An instant afterwards he knocked gently on my door, and entered, carrying a lamp. His face was, as usual, pale as a corpse, but in addition there was a kind of mad hilarity in his eyes. It was a kind of controlled hysteria•. His appearance upset me, but anything was preferable to the solitude that I had experienced. I even welcomed his presence as a relief.

- **adjoining:** that is next to
- **awake:** wake up
- **gasp:** sound when breathing quickly
- **hysteria:** extreme excitement and agitation
- **overpowered:** taken over
- **retiring:** (here) going
- **rustling:** sound that some materials (silk) make
- **struggled:** (here) tried without success
- **swayed fitfully to and fro:** moved quickly backwards and forwards
- **unbearable:** that you can't tolerate

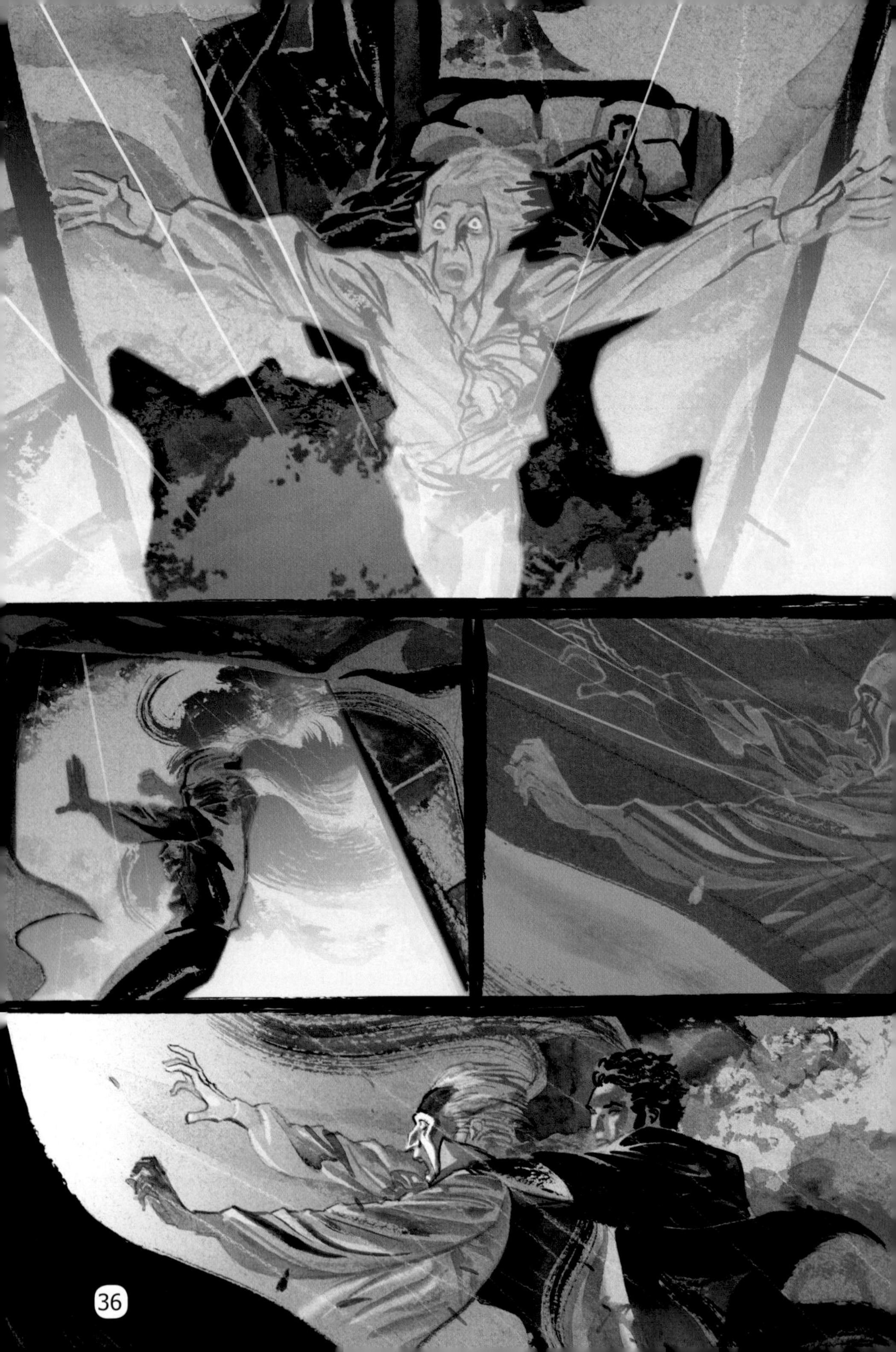

'And have you not seen it?' he said abruptly, after staring around him for some moments in silence. 'Have you not seen it? But, wait! You shall.' After carefully shading• his lamp, he hurried to one of the windows, and threw it open to the storm.

The sudden strength of the gust• of wind that entered nearly lifted us off our feet. It was a stormy night, but it was beautiful and terrible at the same time. A whirlwind• had apparently collected its force in our vicinity•, for there were frequent, violent changes in the direction of the wind. The thickness of the clouds, which were so low that they were pressing upon the towers of the house, did not prevent us from seeing the speed with which they crashed against each other. We had no view of the moon or stars, and no lightning• flashes were visible. But the sky was glowing in the unnatural light of a clearly visible cloud of gas that hung about and covered the house.

'You must not – you shall not see this!' I said to Usher, as I led him, with a gentle violence, from the window to a seat. 'These sights, which confuse you, are just normal electrical phenomena, or perhaps they have their origin in the mist of the lake. Let us close this window. The air is cold and dangerous to your health. Here is one of your favourite romances•. I will read, and you shall listen, and in this way we will pass this terrible night together.'

Glossary

- **gust:** strong rush of wind
- **lightning:** flash of light in the sky
- **romances:** (here) books
- **shading:** protecting with his hand
- **vicinity:** place that is close
- **whirlwind:** wind that moves in fast circles

The old book which I had picked up was the 'Mad Trist' by Sir Launcelot Canning. When I had called it a favourite of Usher's I meant it more as a sad joke than a serious comment. In truth, it is very long and boring and there is little in it that could be interesting for my friend. It was, however, the only book immediately at hand, and I hoped that the excitement that now agitated Usher might find relief in what I read. Judging by the intensity with which he listened, or appeared to listen, to the words of the story, I could congratulate myself on the success of my idea.

Glossary

- **dwelling:** house
- **hermit:** person who lives on their own, away from society
- **hollow-sounding:** that seemed empty
- **mace:** weapon (in left hand above)
- **proceeds:** continues
- **reverberated:** echoed; vibrated
- **ripped:** tore in two
- **spiteful:** who wants to hurt others
- **trist:** secret meeting (usually tryst)

I had arrived at that well-known part of the story where Ethelred, the hero of the Trist, having tried in vain to enter the dwelling• of the hermit• peaceably, proceeds• to enter it by force. The words of the story are as follows:

"And Ethelred, who was by nature a brave man, and who now felt very powerful thanks to the wine that he had drunk, did not wait any longer to speak to the hermit, who was an obstinate and spiteful• man. Feeling the rain upon his shoulders, and fearing the coming storm, he lifted up his mace•, and cracked and ripped• the door, and tore everything apart, so that the noise of the dry and hollow-sounding• wood alarmed and reverberated• throughout the forest."

At the end of this sentence I started, and for a moment, paused; for it appeared to me - although I immediately decided that my excited imagination had deceived me - that I had heard indistinctly, from some very remote part of the house, what might have been the echo (but a low and dull one certainly) of the same cracking and ripping sound which Sir Launcelot had described so exactly. It was, no doubt, the coincidence alone that had drawn my attention, because, in the middle of the rattling of the windows and the ordinary noises of the increasing storm, the sound in itself should not have disturbed me. I continued the story:

"But the good champion Ethelred, now entering the door, was angry and amazed to see no sign of the hermit. Instead of the hermit he saw a huge scaly dragon with a fiery tongue, which sat on guard outside a palace of gold, with a floor of silver. A shield of shining brass hung on the wall, and on it these words were written:

Glossary

- **brass:** metal alloy of copper and zinc
- **champion:** hero
- **conqueror:** winner
- **deceived:** tricked
- **fiery:** with fire
- **scaly:** with scales (small hard plates on the surface of fish, snakes, etc)
- **shield:** metal plate used to protect the body in fighting
- **started:** jumped in shock

Ethelred lifted up his mace, and struck the head of the dragon, which fell before him and died with a cry so horrid• and harsh•, and so piercing•, that Ethelred had to put his hands over his ears to protect them from the dreadful noise, the like of which• he had never heard before." Again I paused abruptly. There could be no doubt that in this instance, I did actually hear – although it was impossible to say from where it came – a low and apparently distant, but harsh, long, and most unusual screaming or grating• sound – exactly as I had imagined the dragon's unnatural shriek• to be.

Although I was shocked by this second most extraordinary coincidence, and I felt confused by my feelings of wonder and extreme terror, I still kept sufficient presence of mind• to avoid alarming my nervous companion by making any observation. I was by no means certain that he had noticed the sounds in question, although during the last few minutes a strange change had certainly taken place in his appearance.

He had gradually moved his chair, so that he was sitting facing the door of the room. I could only partly• see his face, although I saw that his lips were trembling as if he were murmuring inaudibly. His head had dropped down onto his chest, yet, from the wide and rigid opening of the eye as I caught a glance of it in profile, I knew that he was not asleep. The motion of his body, too, conflicted with this idea, because he rocked• from side to side with a gentle yet constant movement.

- **grating:** unpleasant sound like scratching
- **harsh:** hard and cruel
- **horrid:** horrible
- **partly:** not completely
- **piercing:** that penetrates
- **presence of mind:** ability to do the correct things in a crisis
- **rocked:** moved in rhythm
- **shriek:** shout that penetrates
- **the like of which:** something like this

Having rapidly taken notice of all this, I resumed• the narrative of Sir Launcelot, which continued as follows:

"And now, the champion, having escaped from the terrible fury• of the dragon, thinking of the shield, and of breaking the enchantment• which was on it, removed the dragon's body from his path, and walked across the silver pavement• to where the shield was on the wall. It did not wait for his arrival, but fell down upon the silver floor at his feet, with a great and terrible ringing sound."

No sooner had these syllables passed my lips, than - as if at that moment a shield of brass had indeed fallen heavily onto a floor of silver - I became aware of a distant hollow metallic clanging sound, like a muffled• echo.

SENSES

Do you think the narrator has really heard a sound or is it the power of suggestion?
Have you ever thought you heard a sound when there was nothing there?
What was the situation?

Glossary

- **enchantment:** spell; magic formula
- **fury:** great anger
- **muffled:** when a sound is hidden or unclear
- **pavement:** (here) floor
- **resumed:** continued

9 Completely unnerved•, I leapt to my feet; but Usher's rocking movement was undisturbed. I rushed to the chair in which he sat. His eyes were fixed and staring, and his whole face was rigid. But, as I placed my hand upon his shoulder, his whole body shuddered•. A sickly smile trembled on his lips and I saw that he spoke in a low and hurried murmur, as if unconscious of my presence. Bending closely over him, I began to understand the horrible meaning of his words.

• **shuddered:** shook; trembled

• **unnerved:** nervous; anxious; afraid

'Not hear it? Yes, I hear it, and I have heard it. For many minutes, many hours, many days, I have heard it. Yet I did not dare•. Oh, pity me, I am a miserable man! I did not dare. I did not dare to speak! We put her into the tomb while she was still living! Didn't I say that my senses were acute? Now I tell you that I heard her first weak movements in her coffin. I heard them many, many days ago, yet I did not dare to speak! And now tonight … the story of Ethelred! The breaking down of the hermit's door, the death-cry of the dragon, and the clanging of the shield! Instead there was the breaking open of her coffin, the grating of the iron hinges• of her prison, and her struggles inside the vault! Where can I run? Won't she be here soon? Isn't she hurrying to punish me for my haste•? I've heard her footsteps on the stairs. I can hear that heavy and horrible beating of her heart. Mad man!' He jumped to his feet, and screamed out this word, as if in the effort he were giving up his soul. 'Mad man! I tell you that now she is standing outside the door!'

As if his words had the power of a spell•, at that moment the huge doors to which he pointed were thrown open. It was the force of the wind. But there, outside those doors, covered in a shroud•, stood the tall figure of Lady Madeline of Usher. There was blood on her white robes•, and the evidence of a struggle• on every part of her emaciated body. For a moment she remained there, trembling and moving slowly from side to side in the doorway. Then, with a low moaning• cry, she fell heavily onto her brother. And in her final violent dying moment, she brought him to the floor, dead. He was a victim to those terrors that he had predicted•.

Glossary

- **haste:** hurry
- **hinges:** part of a door etc., that allows it to move
- **I did not dare:** I was afraid
- **moaning:** like a low cry
- **predicted:** said what was going to happen
- **robes:** clothes
- **shroud:** cloth that covers a dead person
- **spell:** magic formula
- **struggle:** fight

I ran terrified from that room and from that house. The storm was still in full force as I crossed the old bridge. Suddenly a wild light shone along the path, and I turned to see where it could have come from since only the house and its shadows were behind me. The light was that of the full blood-red moon. It now shone vividly through that once barely visible crack that extended from the roof of the building to its base. As I watched, this crack widened rapidly. In shock I saw the great walls breaking apart. There was a long loud shouting sound like the voice of a thousand waters, and then the deep dark lake closed silently over the fragments of the 'House of Usher'.

After Reading

Personal Response

1 Now that you have read the story, can you say why it is called *The Fall of the House of Usher*?

2 Which part of the story was the most frightening, and why?

3 Would you like to visit the House of Usher? Explain why or why not?

4 What was unusual about the burial of Lady Madeline?

5 Which of the characters do you feel most sympathy for? Explain why.

6 In your opinion what mistakes did Roderick Usher make in his life? Is there anything he could have done to change the course of events? Make a list of suggestions.

After Reading

Comprehension

1 Tick (✓) T (True), F (False) or D (Doesn't say) below.

	T	F	D
a) Was the narrator happy about visiting Roderick Usher?	☐	☐	☐
b) Was the narrator related to Usher?	☐	☐	☐
c) Did Usher have any children?	☐	☐	☐
d) Was Usher in good health?	☐	☐	☐
e) Did the narrator speak to Lady Madeline during his visit?	☐	☐	☐
f) Did the narrator think he could help Usher?	☐	☐	☐
g) Did the doctor check that Lady Madeline was dead?	☐	☐	☐
h) Was Usher sorry that his sister had died?	☐	☐	☐
i) Was the narrator frightened by Usher's behaviour during the storm?	☐	☐	☐
j) Did Usher know that his sister was still alive?	☐	☐	☐
k) Had Usher tried to murder his own sister?	☐	☐	☐
l) Did Lady Madeline kill Usher?	☐	☐	☐

2 Match the words in Column A with the words of similar meaning in Column B.

A	B
mansion	burial
malady	stones
entombment	curtains
physician	house
draperies	sickness
masonry	doctor

3 Here are three summaries of the story. Which is the most accurate and why? Choose one summary and re-write it so that it is closer to the original story.

a) A man goes to stay with his friend Roderick Usher who lives alone with his valet in a large old house. Roderick is sick and disturbed. He is haunted by the ghost of his dead sister Madeline. One night during a fierce storm, Roderick goes completely mad, saying that Madeline was buried alive and that now she has come to take him away. He falls down dead from a heart-attack.

b) A man receives a letter from an old friend, Roderick Usher, inviting him to stay at his house and keep him company. The man hardly recognises Roderick, who is not well physically or mentally. Roderick's sister Madeline dies and Roderick buries her in the vaults of the house. A week later there is a fierce storm. Madeline comes back to life and escapes from her coffin. She finds her brother and kills him.

c) A man visits his old friend Roderick Usher. Both Roderick and his sister Madeline are sick. The man keeps Roderick company and tries to cheer him up, but Madeline dies while he is staying at the house. He helps Roderick bury her body. During a storm, Madeline appears in the house after escaping from her coffin. In reality she had been asleep and Roderick had buried her alive. Madeline collapses dead on top of her brother and he dies instantly.

4 Talk about a place where you have had to stay.
Describe:

a) Why you were there.

b) What your room was like.

c) The sensations you had going into the place and if you would like to live there.

After Reading

Characters

1 **Work with a partner. What facts do you know about the narrator, Roderick, and Madeline? Write two sentences about each of these characters.**

2 **Here is an extract from a police report describing Roderick Usher. See if you can complete it using information from the story.**

People who knew Roderick Usher said that he had changed a lot in recent years. They say that his skin was as .... as that of a .... His eyes had become .... and.......... . In fact people found the .... of his skin and the .... look of his eyes quite startling. His lips were said to be .... and very.......... . He had a .... nose, but his .... were broad. His .... was finely-shaped and he had a .... forehead. His hair could be described as.............., and .... like a web, but it was also very .... and.......... . Judging by his appearance he did not seem at all ....

3 **Do you think that Roderick Usher is mad? Look for evidence in the story to support your theory. Make a list of any behaviour that seems normal or abnormal to you.**

4 At the beginning of the story we learn that Roderick Usher has written a letter to his friend asking him to come and stay at the House of Usher. Use the information from the story to write Usher's letter of invitation.

Begin like this:

My dear friend,
It has been many years since our last meeting …

End the letter like this:

I look forward to your response,
Your most affectionate friend,
Roderick

5 'Lady Madeline's disease had puzzled her doctors for a long time'. What were her symptoms and what was their probable cause? Imagine you are her doctor. Write a report about the state of her health Give your advice for her recovery.

The causes of Lady Madeline's illness are not entirely clear …

6 Choose one of the characters in the story - Roderick Usher, Lady Madeline or the narrator. Write a sequence of entries from this character's diary explaining the events of the story from his/her point of view. Work individually or with a partner.

After Reading

Plot and Theme

1 Put these events from the story in the correct order.

a) [1] Arriving at the House of Usher the narrator discovers that his friend Roderick Usher is sick.
b) [ ] There is a storm and the narrator cannot sleep.
c) [ ] Usher and the narrator bury Lady Madeline in a coffin in the house's vaults.
d) [ ] Lady Madeline appears in the doorway.
e) [ ] The narrator learns that Usher's sister Madeline has a strange disease.
f) [ ] Usher and the narrator pass the time reading and painting.
g) [ ] The narrator escapes but the house falls apart and breaks into fragments.
h) [ ] Usher and the narrator hear screams.
i) [ ] Lady Madeline dies and falls on Usher, killing him.
j) [ ] The narrator tries to calm Usher by reading to him.
k) [ ] Usher tells the narrator that Lady Madeline is dead.

2 What is the main theme of the book? In groups read and discuss the list of possible themes below. Are any of these the theme of the *Fall of the House of Usher*? If not, write your own summary of the theme.

a) Forces that we do not understand control our destiny.
b) Sooner or later people pay for the wrong-doings of their ancestors.
c) Objects are like living things and have a life of their own.
d) Isolation from the world brings death.
e) What we believe will happen, does really happen.

3 **Some of the objects and events in *The Fall of the House of Usher* have a symbolic meaning. Can you match the items on the left with the ideas on the right?**

a) ☐ The crumbling state of the house
b) ☐ The lake that reflects the house
c) ☐ The storm
d) ☐ The house's empty windows
e) ☐ The bridge outside the house

1 The emptiness of life in the House of Usher
2 A link with the outside world
3 Usher's image as reflected in his twin sister
4 The decaying state of the Usher family
5 Usher's madness

4 **Have you noticed any other parts of the story that may have a symbolic meaning?**

5 **What part does the weather play in the story? Imagine you are reporting on the storm in the story. Describe it in a short weather report for the local newspaper. Use some of the notes:**

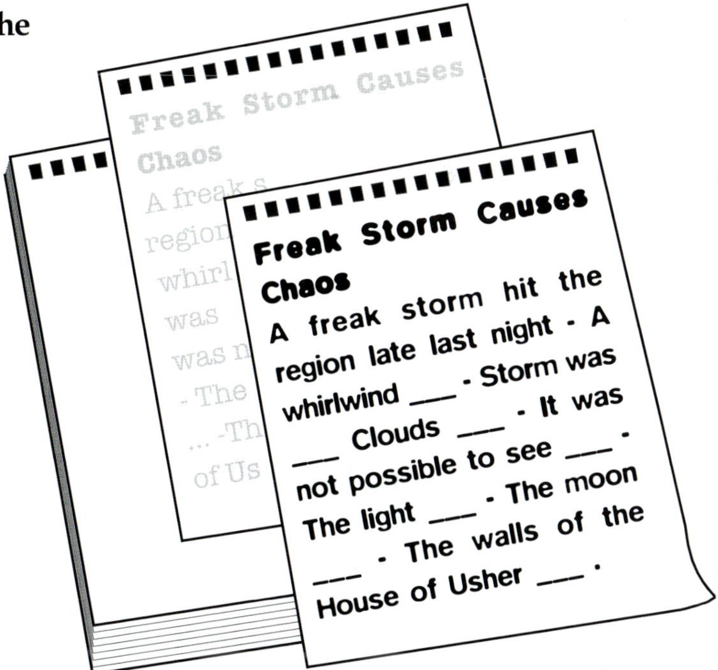

After Reading

Test

1 **Listen to a detective questioning the narrator about events at the House of Usher. Then tick (✓) the correct statements.**

1 a) ☐ There was a crack in the back wall of the house.
b) ☐ There was a crack in the front wall of the house.
2 a) ☐ He could only listen to piano music.
b) ☐ He couldn't listen to anything other than stringed instruments.
3 a) ☐ Madeline was entombed in the family grave yard.
b) ☐ Roderick entombed Madeline in an old dungeon.
4 a) ☐ The narrator heard Lady Madeline escaping from the vault.
b) ☐ The narrator didn't hear Lady Madeline escaping from the vault.

2 **Read the questions and tick (✓) the correct answers.**

a) **When the narrator arrived at the House of Usher, he found his friend Roderick incoherent. Why was he incoherent?**
1 ☐ He was very nervous.
2 ☐ He was drunk.
3 ☐ He had been drugged.
4 ☐ He was emotional.

b) **Roderick had a terrible fear. What was it?**
1 ☐ a fear of water
2 ☐ a fear of danger
3 ☐ a fear of death
4 ☐ a fear of disease

c) What was the narrator impressed by?

1 ☐ Roderick's paintings
2 ☐ Roderick's guitar playing
3 ☐ Roderick's song lyrics
4 ☐ Roderick's dancing

d) How did the narrator feel when Roderick came to his room on his last night at the House of Usher?

1 ☐ terrified
2 ☐ relieved not to be alone any more
3 ☐ miserable
4 ☐ angry

3 **Get into pairs. Student A look at the picture on page 21. What relevance does it have to the story? What can you see in the picture? Tell Student B.**

Student B look at the picture on page 45. What relevance does it have to the story? What can you see in the picture? Tell Student A.

4 **You have just read *The Fall of the House of Usher*. Write a book report describing the story.**

- Say what kind of story it is.
- Describe the setting and characters.
- Summarize the plot.
- Give opinions on the story and characters.
- Would you recommend the story to a friend?

After Reading

Test

1 Read the text below and choose the most suitable word for each space.

Roderick's **(a)** .... sister, Madeline was seriously ill when Roderick's friend arrived at the House of Usher. Roderick was very upset because Madeline was his only **(b)** .... relative and he was afraid she would die. Doctors **(c)** .... by her illness. Her body was wasting away and she **(d)** .... fell into a deep sleep.
One evening, Roderick told his friend that his sister **(e)** .... He wanted to keep his dead sister in a coffin in a vault for two weeks and then bury her in the family's burial ground.
However, Madeline wasn't dead and seven or eight days later, in the **(f)** .... of a terrible storm, she escaped from her tomb and climbed the stairs to the room **(g)** .... Roderick and his friend sat. For a moment, the pale emaciated woman stood in the doorway and then she died, **(h)** .... her brother and killing him.

a)	**1** twin	**2** older	**3** younger	**4** half
b)	**1** livelier	**2** lively	**3** life	**4** living
c)	**1** are puzzled	**2** puzzled	**3** were puzzled	**4** have puzzled
d)	**1** never	**2** frequently	**3** almost	**4** fairly
e)	**1** had died	**2** died	**3** dead	**4** is dying
f)	**1** duration	**2** time	**3** middle	**4** end
g)	**1** that	**2** which	**3** where	**4** when
h)	**1** fell on	**2** falling on	**3** fall on	**4** had fallen on

The Oval Portrait

About the Book

The Oval Portrait was first published in 1842 as *Life in Death.* Poe subsequently• edited• and cut the story and it was republished as *The Oval Portrait* three years later. It is one of Poe's shortest stories but includes themes that recur through many of his works such as death and monomania (a type of paranoia• where the sufferer is obsessed with a single idea or emotion). Elements from the story inspired Oscar Wilde's novel, *The Portrait of Dorian Gray.*

The Oval Portrait is a story within a story. It starts with an injured narrator taking refuge• for the night in an abandoned mansion in the mountains. He is drawn• to the paintings in the room where he is sleeping and finds a book that describes them. One painting in particular strikes• him and when he reads about it in the book his interest is explained.

The story focuses on the relationship between art and life. In the story art and life are rivals. An extreme obsession with art can lead to death, as art takes the vital forces from life in the creative process.

Extreme obsession (monomania) is recurrent• in many of Poe's tales. In *The Fall of the House of Usher* Roderick Usher is ruined by his own fear. In *The Masque of the Red Death* Prince Prospero's obsession with the disease, the Red Death, ultimately leads to his own death.

Glossary

- **drawn:** (here) attracted
- **edited:** changed and corrected a piece of writing before it was published
- **paranoia:** obsessive and unreasonable fear
- **recurrent:** repeated
- **strikes:** (here) gets his interest
- **subsequently:** at a later stage
- **taking refuge:** going somewhere safe

Before Reading

1 Look at these pictures from the story. Write six questions about them. Exchange questions with your partner. Then, write answers to your partner's questions. Keep these answers in a safe place.

2 What do you think *The Oval Portrait* will be about? Tick (✓) below.

a) ☐ A man who meets the woman of his dreams
b) ☐ The story of an old house
c) ☐ A man who is afraid of the dark
d) ☐ An unhappy love story
e) ☐ The story of someone who appears in a painting
f) ☐ A ghost story

12 **3 Listen to the start of the story. Tick (✓) T (True) or F (False).**

	T	F
a) The narrator is called Pedro.	☐	☐
b) The narrator is hurt.	☐	☐
c) They do not have the owner's permission to enter the house.	☐	☐
d) No one had lived in the house for a long time.	☐	☐
e) The room they went to was very austere.	☐	☐
f) The narrator was struck by the paintings.	☐	☐

1 **Imagine that you have to stay alone in an old house. Describe what it looks like. You decide to sleep in one of the house's bedrooms. Describe the room. Tell your story to the other students in your group. Whose story was the best?**

2 **Here are some words that appear in the story. Match them to their definitions.**

a)	☐	abandoned	1	hated the thought of
b)	☐	surrounded	2	left empty, not repaired, and not taken care of
c)	☐	gazed	3	fooled or cheated
d)	☐	entranced	4	were all around
e)	☐	dreaded	5	hypnotised; fascinated
f)	☐	deceived	6	looked for a period of time

3 **Use the words to complete these sentences.**

a) The house seemed to have been .... quite recently.

b) The only things she .... were the tools that stole her lover from her.

c) I wanted to make sure that my sight had not .... me.

d) I asked Pedro to open the black velvet curtains that .... the bed.

e) For a very long time I read, and I .... at the paintings.

f) For one moment, the painter stood .... before his work.

4 Take a look at the woman in the painting. Think about the following questions. Then imagine you are the woman and write a short presentation of yourself. (Approximately 3 minutes). Give the presentation in class.

a) Who do you think she is?
b) What is her name?
c) How old is she?
d) Where does she live?
e) What are her likes and dislikes?
f) In what period is she living?
g) Why is she the subject of the painting?

5 Match the following genres to the paintings below. Choose one of the genres and use the Internet to find out as much about it as possible. Write a report.

a) Pop Art b) Still life c) Landscape d) Portrait

1 ☐ 

2 ☐ 

3 ☐ 

4 ☐ 

6 Now as you read the story note the answers to these questions:

a) Where does the story take place?
b) What did the narrator find on his pillow?
c) Where did the painter work?

7 Make up another three questions to ask your partner, after they have finished reading.

13 After my accident, my servant Pedro broke into• an empty house so that I would have a place to shelter and would not have to spend the night in the open air. We were in the Apennine mountains and the house we had found was both grand and gloomy•. It seemed to have been abandoned quite recently. We made ourselves comfortable in one of the smallest rooms that was not as sumptuously furnished• as the others. It lay in a remote tower of the building. Its decorations were rich, yet tattered• and old. Tapestries and weapons covered the walls, together with a very large number of lively modern paintings in rich gold frames. These paintings hung on all the main walls of the house but also in its many corners. I was slightly delirious• and this is probably why the paintings drew my attention.

THE ACCIDENT

Have you ever had an accident or been ill while you were away from home?
What happened?
What kind of accident do you think the narrator had?

Glossary

- **broke into:** entered a place without permission
- **delirious:** confused because he has a fever
- **gloomy:** dark and depressing
- **sumptuously furnished:** furnished in a rich and grand style
- **tattered:** torn; in rags

Since it was already night, I asked Pedro to close the heavy shutters• of the room, to light the candles, and to open the black velvet curtains that surrounded the bed. I wanted all this to be done so that even if I couldn't sleep, I could at least look at these pictures and read through the small volume• that I had found on my pillow, which discussed and described them in detail.

For a very long time I read, and I gazed• at the paintings. The hours passed and midnight came. I did not like the position of the candelabrum•, but rather than disturb my sleeping servant, I stretched out my hand with difficulty and moved it so that it threw its rays more fully on the book that I was reading.

This action produced an effect that I had not expected. The rays of the numerous candles now fell on a corner of the room that had previously been in the shadow. Because of this I saw in vivid• light a picture that I had not noticed before. It was the portrait of a young girl who was just ripening• into womanhood. I glanced• at the painting, and then closed my eyes. I was not sure why I did this. It was an impulsive movement and I wanted to make sure that my sight had not deceived me. In a few moments I looked again fixedly• at the painting.

Glossary

- **candelabrum:** a metal holder for candles
- **fixedly:** for a long time; intently; with steady attention
- **gazed:** looked for a period of time
- **glanced:** looked quickly
- **ripening:** maturing; becoming (a woman)
- **shutters:** outer covers for windows
- **vivid:** strong
- **volume:** book

Now I was wide awake and sure of what I had seen. The portrait, I have already said, was that of a young girl. It was a painting of her head and shoulders, done in what is technically termed a 'vignette•' manner. The arms, the chest, and even the ends of her radiant hair melted into the deep shadow that formed the background of the whole picture. The painting's frame was oval, richly gilded• and very ornate•. As a work of art nothing could be more admirable than the painting itself, but it was not the skill of the painting or the immortal beauty of the face that had made such an impression on me. Nor had I mistaken the head for that of a living person. Thinking earnestly• upon these points. I remained, for an hour perhaps, half sitting, half reclining•, with my eyes fixed on the portrait. Eventually, I felt I understood the true secret of its effect and I fell back into the bed.

- **earnestly:** seriously
- **gilded:** covered in gold paint
- **ornate:** highly decorated
- **reclining:** lying down
- **vignette:** a painting or drawing of someone's head and shoulders

I had found that the spell• of the picture was due to the expression on the face, which was so lifelike and alive. At first I found it shocking, then it confused me and then finally it horrified me. With a sense of deep and reverent• admiration I returned the candelabrum to its former position. Now that the cause of my agitation was out of sight, I looked for the volume that discussed the paintings and their histories. Turning to the description that identified the oval portrait, I read the following:

"She was a young woman of great beauty and full of joy. It was an evil time when she saw, loved, and married the painter. He was passionate, studious, and austere•, and he was already married to his love of painting. She was beautiful and full of joy, all light and smiles. She loved all things, hating only the art of painting, which was her rival. The only things she dreaded• were the pallet• and the brushes and the other tools that stole her lover from her. For this reason it was a terrible thing for this lady to hear the painter say that he wanted to paint her.

But she was obedient, and she sat meekly• for many weeks in the dark room of a high tower, where the light fell from above onto the pale canvas• of the painting. The painter loved his work, which continued from hour to hour, and from day to day. He was a wild and moody• man, who became so lost in his dreams that he did not see that the health and spirits of his bride were affected. She pined• visibly to all but him.

Glossary

- **austere:** serious
- **canvas:** material used for painting on
- **dreaded:** hated the thought of
- **meekly:** obediently; without complaining
- **moody:** inclined to become angry or sad
- **pallet:** a piece of wood on which the painter mixes his paint
- **pined:** became pale and thin
- **reverent:** respectful and religious
- **spell:** intense fascination

PORTRAITS

Do you like having your photograph taken?
Would you like to have your portrait painted?
Why did the young bride not want to have her portrait painted?

Yet his bride smiled on and on without complaining because she could see that the painter (who was well-known) took such pleasure in his work. He worked day and night to paint the woman who loved him so much. Yet she grew weaker and more dispirited every day. Some people who saw the portrait spoke in low voices of how marvellous it was, and how it was proof of the painter's deep love for her. As his work came to an end, the painter admitted• no one into the tower. He had grown wild with passion for his work, and he rarely looked away from the canvas even to look at the face of his wife. He did not see that the tints• that he spread on the canvas were taken from the cheeks of the woman who sat beside him. Many weeks had passed, and very little remained to do, except for one brushstroke on the mouth and one tint on the eye. The brush was applied, and then the tint was placed.

- **admitted:** let enter
- **tints:** colours

OBSESSIONS

Do you think that people can become obsessed with their work, their studies or their hobbies?
Can you think of any examples?
Has this ever happened to you?

For one moment, the painter stood entranced• before his work, but the next moment, while he was still staring at the painting, he started to tremble with terror and turned very white. He cried out in a loud voice, 'This is indeed life itself!' Then he turned suddenly to look at his beloved: she was dead!"

Glossary

- **entranced:** hypnotised; fascinated

After Reading

Personal Response

1 **How much of the story of *The Oval Portrait* did you guess just by looking at the pictures? Look at the answers that you wrote to your partner's questions before reading the story. Compare them with what you have just read.**

2 **Look again at *Before Reading Exercise 2 (page 59)*. Which statement correctly summarises what the story is about? Give reasons for your answer.**

3 **The narrator sheltered in the house because he had had an accident. Can you guess what might have happened to him? Have you ever hurt yourself in an accident? Where were you? What happened? Who helped you? Work in a group. Tell the other students about your experience.**

4 **Do you feel sorry for the young woman in the portrait? Why? Why not?**
What advice would you have given her? Write her a short letter. Begin like this:

5 **Discuss the following questions and give reasons for your answers:**
- Is this a good story?
- Does any part of it frighten you?
- What would you do to improve the story?
- Can you think of a different ending?

After Reading

Comprehension

1 Read these statements about *The Oval Portrait* and tick (✓) T (True), F (False) or D (Doesn't say) below. Discuss your answers with the students in your group. Do you all have the same answers?

	T	F	D
a) The narrator and Pedro chose to stay in the largest room in the house.	☐	☐	☐
b) The narrator learned about the painting from a description in a book.	☐	☐	☐
c) The young woman and her husband were very similar in character.	☐	☐	☐
d) When the painter was working on the portrait, people visited the house.	☐	☐	☐
e) The young woman was afraid of her husband.	☐	☐	☐
f) The painter painted his wife's portrait because he loved her.	☐	☐	☐

2 Study the sentences below that are taken from the text. Find these sentences in the story, then explain what the underlined words refer to.

a) <u>It</u> lay in a remote tower of the building.
b) I was not sure why I did <u>this</u>.
c) At first I found <u>it</u> shocking, then <u>it</u> confused me and then finally <u>it</u> horrified me.
d) "<u>This</u> is indeed life <u>itself</u>!"

3 Explain the following questions to a partner using your own words.

a) Why did the narrator find the painting shocking?
b) Why did the young woman dread the painter's pallet and brushes?
c) Why did the painter not notice that his young wife was ill?
d) Why did the painter tremble when he saw the finished painting?

4 Join the pairs of sentences below to make one sentence containing a defining or non-defining relative clause. Look at the examples below.

The main tools were the pallet and the brushes. The painter used them.
The main tools that the painter used were the pallet and the brushes.

The painting took a long time to complete. It was perfect.
The painting, which took a long time to complete, was perfect.

a) Pedro was the narrator's servant. He broke into the empty house.

....

b) The house was abandoned. It was the painter's old house.

....

c) The narrator read the book. He had found it on his pillow.

....

d) The painter was lost in his dreams. He was a moody man.

....

e) The people saw the portrait. They said it looked like the painter's wife.

....

f) The young woman became weak and depressed. She was once full of energy.

....

After Reading

Characters

1 **Write the words and phrases under the correct person or object.**

The Narrator	The Painter	The Painter's Wife	The Painting

admirable alive confused curious delirious
full of energy fun-loving humble lifelike
moody obedient obsessed studious
startling wide awake wild

2 **Imagine you are the narrator and that you have access to the Internet. Write an e-mail home saying that you had an accident, explaining how it happened and how you feel.**

Send Chat Attach Address Font Colors Save As Draft

To:

Cc:

Subject:

Account: Sign:

Hi everyone,
Sorry for not being in contact, but I've had a small accident. Don't worry it's nothing serious. Yesterday afternoon I …

3 **We are told that the painter 'had become obsessed with his work'. What does he do that shows his obsession?**

4 **Who in the story might have said the following words?**

a) 'Go away! You can't come in here any more!'
b) 'This is so lifelike!'
c) 'Please, don't worry about me, I am fine.'
d) 'Pedro, could you close the shutters of the room?'
e) 'I have to paint you.'
f) 'He must be deeply in love with his wife.'

5 **Rewrite the sentences above in reported speech. Use these verbs:**

exclaim insist refuse ask declare persuade

Example:
'Go away! You can't come in here any more!'
The painter refused to let his visitors come in any more.

6 **Work with a partner and invent the rest of the conversations around each quote. Role-play them in class.**

7 **Imagine you are the painter. Explain what happened. Defend yourself by explaining what happened from your point of view.**

After Reading

Plot and Theme

1 ***The Oval Portrait* is really a 'story within a story'. Do you agree? If so, what titles would you give to:**

a) **The story ....**
b) **The story within the story ....**

2 **Put the following sentences in the correct order:**

a) [1] The narrator and his servant made themselves comfortable in an abandoned house.
b) [ ] He looked up the description of this oval portrait in the book and read it.
c) [ ] The painter did not allow anyone to enter the place where he was working.
d) [ ] When he finally finished his painting, he discovered that his wife was dead.
e) [ ] His wife's health was affected, but he did not notice.
f) [ ] At one point, he noticed a very lifelike portrait in the corner of the room.
g) [ ] A beautiful young woman married a painter, but he was obsessed with his work.
h) [ ] As he worked on her portrait day after day, she became weak and depressed.
i) [ ] The paintings on the walls of the house fascinated the narrator.
j) [ ] On his pillow he found a book that contained descriptions of these paintings.
k) [ ] One day the painter decided to paint a portrait of his bride.

3 Which of the following do you most agree with? Put them in order of importance to you.

a) ☐ Art is more important than life because it lasts forever.
b) ☐ Art is different from life and we should not confuse the two.
c) ☐ We should value life more than art.
d) ☐ Life is imperfect, but art is always perfect.
e) ☐ Art is in competition with life, and since art is better, it always wins.
f) ☐ Art is important because it lives on after death.
g) ☐ When art copies life, it steals something from life.
h) ☐ The painter was right to love his painting more than his wife.
i) ☐ The painter's wife died because she was too beautiful.
j) ☐ Art helps us to remember the beauty of the past.

4 Find an English language newspaper and study some of the headlines. Can you guess the content of the stories they relate to? Read *The Oval Portrait* headlines below. What do you think they refer to?

a) **ARTIST ACCUSED OF WIFE'S DEATH**

b) **POLICE ARREST APENNINE HOUSE BURGLARS**

c) **Painter kidnapped our daughter, claim bride's family**

d) **INJURED MAN FOUND SAFE**

5 Can you invent some similar headlines of your own?

6 Choose one of the newspaper headlines above and, working with a partner, write a short article related to the events of the story.

After Reading

Test

1 **Can you remember the story? Fill in the missing information in the numbered spaces.**

a) The portrait hung in an (1) .... house in the Apennine (2) ....
b) The narrator of the story was with his (3) ...., Pedro when he saw the portrait.
c) Large (4) .... hung on all the main walls of the gloomy old house.
d) The portrait fascinated the narrator because it was very (5) ....
e) The narrator learnt all about the portrait from a little book on his (6) ....

14 2 **Now listen to the conversation and check your answers.**

3 **The *Mona Lisa* is a famous portrait. Write an entry about the *Mona Lisa* for the little book that the narrator of the story found. You can use the Internet to help you. Think of the following questions.**

- Who was *Mona Lisa*?
- Who painted her?
- What is special about the portrait?
- Where is it now?
- What do you think of the *Mona Lisa*?

4 Read the statements below about the story. Tick (✓) T (True) or F (False).

	T	F
a) The oval portrait of the girl had a simple gold frame.	☐	☐
b) The portrait made an impression on the narrator because it was very skilfully painted.	☐	☐
c) The narrator was not sure why he was so drawn to the painting.	☐	☐
d) The narrator was shocked by the lifelike quality of the portrait.	☐	☐
e) The girl shared her husband's passion for art.	☐	☐
f) The girl was very happy when her husband said that he wanted to paint her.	☐	☐

5 Work in pairs. Student A look at Portrait A. What can you see in the picture? What does the picture tell you about the woman? What style is used to portray the woman? Imagine you are the woman, introduce yourself to Student B and tell each other about yourselves.

Student B look at Portrait B. What can you see in the picture? What does the picture tell you about the woman? What style is used to portray the woman? How are the pictures different?

A

B

After Reading

Test

1 **Read the questions and tick (✓) the most suitable answer to each one.**

a) Who noticed that the painter's wife was growing weaker and weaker?
1 ☐ nobody
2 ☐ everybody but the painter
3 ☐ her family
4 ☐ his family

b) Why didn't the girl complain?
1 ☐ She was happy so she said nothing.
2 ☐ She enjoyed being painted.
3 ☐ Her husband never listened to her complaints.
4 ☐ She loved her husband and she knew he really enjoyed painting.

c) What happened to the girl's cheeks as the artist painted her?
1 ☐ They grew redder and healthier.
2 ☐ They disappeared.
3 ☐ They grew paler and lost their colour.
4 ☐ They grew brighter and she looked happier.

d) What did the painter realize in the end?
1 ☐ The painting was terrible.
2 ☐ The painting was in fact real. It had sucked the life out of his wife.
3 ☐ The painting didn't look like his wife.
4 ☐ The painting wasn't as beautiful as his wife.

The Masque of the Red Death

About the Book

The Masque of the Red Death was first published in 1842 and it is an allegorical• tale about the inevitability of death. The story uses many features of Gothic fiction such as physical and psychological fear, castles, feudal society• and death.

The story is set in an unnamed time and place. A terrible disease, the Red Death, is spreading• rapidly throughout the land, killing everyone it meets. Prince Prospero, along with one thousand noble friends, escapes to an isolated abbey where he is sure they will be happy and safe. After several months he organises a fancy dress ball in a set of rooms that have been decorated in different colours. The last room is decorated in black and has a black clock that rings every hour. However on the stroke of midnight• an uninvited guest arrives, dressed as the Red Death.

The story is a very good example of Poe's Gothic horror short stories. Poe creates a dark and uneasy atmosphere and the story focuses on images of blood and death, while the personification of the Red Death adds an element of the supernatural. *The Masque of the Red Death* also reflects Poe's vision of what a short story should be like. According to Poe, a short story should be so well written that every word, from beginning to end, contributes to the overall effect. In this story a series of powerful symbolic images and an impeccable• narrative voice are tightly woven• into a macabre tale of horror with great insight into the human condition.

Glossary

- **allegorical:** containing an allegory (a book, story etc where ideas are represented by people, images, etc.)
- **feudal society:** a society of rich landowners and poor farmers
- **impeccable:** perfect; without fault
- **spreading:** covering; distributing itself
- **stroke of midnight:** exactly midnight
- **woven:** (here) integrated

Before Reading

1 Work with a partner. Look at these illustrations from the book for two minutes. Close the book, and write down all the words and phrases associated with the illustrations that you can think of.

2 Choose one of the illustrations and, using your words, describe what is happening in the picture. Add and invent details if you wish.

3 Give your story to a partner and get them to continue it, predicting what is going to happen next.
Share your stories with the rest of the class.

4 Look quickly through the illustrations in the book. Do they have anything in common? What atmosphere do they suggest? What elements in the illustrations contribute to the atmosphere (subject, colour, light, style, etc.)?

1 Listen to Prince Prospero then answer the questions below.

a) Who is he speaking to?
b) What is happening in the country?
c) Where does he want to go?
d) What supplies does he take with him?

2 Based on the listening, choose two adjectives from the list below that describe Prince Prospero. Tell a partner why you think they are the most suitable.

a) ☐ careful
b) ☐ charitable
c) ☐ generous
d) ☐ foolish
e) ☐ frightened
f) ☐ fun
g) ☐ imprudent
h) ☐ optimistic

3 Prince Prospero organises a 'masked ball' for his friends. Imagine that you are planning a party. Prepare a checklist of all the things that you have to do. Now design an invitation to your party.

4 **Colours have symbolic meaning in the story. What do you associate with the following colours? You can choose from the list below or add your own ideas.**

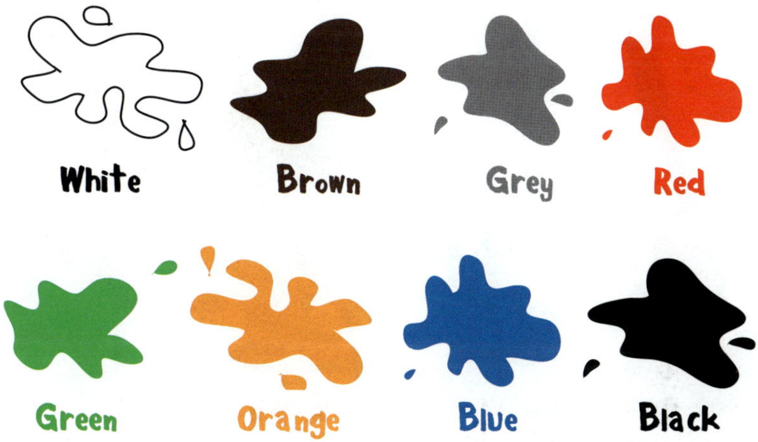

balance	death	hope	money	power
blood	dirt	jealousy	mystery	purity
boredom	elegance	life	nature	sadness
creativity	energy	love	passion	tradition
danger	happiness	luck	peace	warmth

5 **Close your eyes and think of a person or thing that you associate with each colour. Write a sentence about each one.**

6 **What do you think the *Red Death* of the story's title refers to? Perhaps you have already guessed. Talk to your partner and find out if you have the same answer. Now read the first two sentences of the story to find out if you were correct.**

17 For a long time the 'Red Death' had devastated the country. No pestilence• had ever been so fatal, or so terrible. It started and ended in the blood – in the redness and the horror of blood. There were sharp pains, and sudden dizziness, and then heavy bleeding from the pores• of the skin, and then death. Red marks upon the body and especially on the face of the victim were sure signs of the disease. The whole attack, progress and termination of the disease lasted half an hour.

THE RED DEATH

Why is this disease called the Red Death?
What do you think might have caused it?
What is the best way to control or cure diseases like this?
What infectious diseases exist today and how are we dealing with them?

Glossary

- **pestilence:** plague; infectious disease
- **pores:** small holes in the surface of the skin

But Prince Prospero was happy and fearless and wise. When his territories were half empty, he called into his presence a thousand healthy and cheerful friends from among the knights and ladies of his court, and with these he retired to the isolation of one of his fortified• abbeys•. This was an extensive and magnificent place, the creation of the prince's own eccentric yet grand taste.

A strong, high wall circled it. This wall had iron gates. The servants, using furnaces• and hammers, welded• the bolts• of the gates. They intended to leave no means of entry or exit if inside there were sudden signs of despair or panic. The abbey had plenty of supplies•. By taking these precautions the courtiers defended themselves against the possibility of infection. The external world could take care of itself. In the meantime it was foolish to feel sorry, or to think. The prince had provided everything that would give pleasure. There were fools, there were entertainers, there were ballet dancers, there were musicians, there was beauty, there was wine. All this, and security, were inside. Outside was the 'Red Death'.

PRINCE PROSPERO

What kind of person is Prince Prospero?
Do you agree that he is 'happy and fearless and wise'?
Does his name have any special significance?
Where would you choose to be – inside the abbey with Prince Prospero or outside risking the danger of infection by the 'Red Death'?

Glossary

- **abbeys:** buildings where monks live
- **bolts:** locks
- **fortified:** made strong in order to protect it
- **furnaces:** fires for heating metal
- **supplies:** (here) food and drink
- **welded:** sealed or joined by heating the metal

It was towards the close of the fifth or sixth month of his isolation, while outside the pestilence was at its worst, that Prince Prospero entertained his thousand friends at a splendid masked ball•.

It was an impressive scene, that masquerade•. But first let me tell you of the rooms in which it was held. There were seven of these - a magnificent suite•. In many palaces the rooms in these suites are in a long straight line, and the doors slide• back nearly to the walls on both sides, so that all the rooms can be clearly seen. Here the case was very different, as was typical of the prince's love of bizarre things.

The rooms were built in such an irregular way that it was only possible to see one room at a time. There was a sharp• turn every twenty or thirty yards•, and at each turn there was a new effect. To the right and the left, in the middle of each wall, a tall, narrow Gothic• window looked onto a closed corridor that followed the twists and turns of the suite. These windows were of stained glass•. Their colour matched the decorations of the room into which they opened. The room at the eastern extremity, for example, was decorated in blue - and its windows were vividly blue.

- **Gothic:** a style of European architecture popular between 12th and 16th centuries
- **masked ball:** a dance for which people wear colourful masks that hide their identity
- **masquerade:** a dance or ball at which people wear masks and costumes
- **sharp:** (here) abrupt; acute
- **slide:** move smoothly
- **stained glass**: coloured glass often used in the windows of churches
- **suite:** a set or a group of rooms
- **yards:** one yard is equal to 0.9144 metres

The second room had purple ornaments and tapestries, and here the glass in the windows was purple. The third room was green, and so were the windows. The fourth was furnished and lit with orange – the fifth with white – the sixth with violet. The seventh apartment was covered in black velvet tapestries that hung all over the ceiling and down the walls, falling in heavy folds on a carpet of the same material and colour. But in this room only, the colour of the windows was not the same as the decorations. The window panes here were scarlet, a deep blood colour.

There were no lamps or candle holders in any of the seven rooms. There was no light of any kind from lamps or candles inside the rooms. But in the corridors that followed the suite, a heavy tripod, carrying a brazier of fire, stood opposite each window. The rays of the fire illuminated the room brightly through the tinted glass, and this produced a multitude of colourful and fantastic effects. But in the western or black room the effect of the fire's light shining through the blood-tinted panes on to the dark tapestries, was ghastly in the extreme. And it produced such a wild look on the faces of those who entered, that very few of the company were courageous enough to set foot inside it.

NUMBERS AND COLOURS

What is your lucky number?
What is your favourite colour?
What is the significance of numbers and colours in the story?
Work with a partner and compare your ideas. Then, search the Internet for further information about the meaning of numbers and colours.

Glossary

- **brazier:** a portable fire of hot coals
- **ghastly in the extreme:** especially horrible or terrifying
- **panes:** sheets of glass
- **tapestries:** wool or cloth pictures

In this room there also stood against the western wall a gigantic clock made of ebony•. Its pendulum• swung back and forward with a dull, heavy, monotonous clang•. When the minute hand had circled the clock's face, and the hour struck, a clear, loud, deep and exceedingly musical sound came from the clock. It was such a strange sound that, at the end of each hour, the musicians of the orchestra had to pause, momentarily, in their performance, to listen to the sound. Because of this the dancers had to stop their evolutions•, and the enjoyment of the whole company was interrupted.

While the chimes• of the clock were still ringing, the most energetic dancers grew pale, and the older and more sedate• ones seemed confused or thoughtful. But when the echoes of the chimes had stopped, laughter immediately spread through the group.

- **chimes:** ringing sound of a bell or clock
- **clang:** sound of metal
- **ebony:** hard black wood
- **evolutions:** spinning; turning in circles
- **pendulum:** something that swings
- **sedate:** calm; dignified

The musicians looked at each other and smiled as if they were smiling at their own nervousness and foolishness. And they whispered to each other that the next time the clock chimed it would not affect them again in the same way. Then, after a lapse• of sixty minutes, (just three thousand, six hundred seconds later) the clock chimed once more and there were the same feelings of concern, agitation and wonder• as before.

TIME

Do you wear a watch?
How often do you check it?
How important is time in your life?
How does time play a role in the story?
How is time represented?
What is Edgar Allen Poe telling us about the subject of time?

In spite of these things, it was a cheerful and magnificent party. The tastes of the prince were strange. He had a fine eye for colours and effects. His plans were bold, and his ideas were wild. Some people might have thought he was mad. His followers felt that he was not. For this party he had organised the decoration of the seven rooms himself, and he had also suggested how the guests should dress. They had a grotesque• appearance.

Glossary

- **grotesque:** strange and ugly
- **lapse:** period of time that has passed
- **wonder:** marvel; thoughtfulness

There was much glare• and glitter• and energy and fantasy. There were strangely dressed figures and odd costumes that seemed the work of a madman. Much was beautiful, wild, bizarre, and terrible, and there was also much that might have produced feelings of disgust.

- **glare:** excessive brightness
- **glitter:** when something is shining

Dancing through the seven rooms to the wild music of the orchestra, there was a multitude of fantastic characters, coloured by the light from the windows. And then the ebony clock, standing in the black velvet hall, struck. For a moment everything was still and silent except for the voice of the clock. The dancers seemed to freeze. But when the echoes of the chime died away there was laughter. After the music returned, the dream-like figures continued dancing back and forth• more merrily than ever. But none of the dancers entered the seventh room. The night was fading and a red light flowed through the room's blood-coloured panes, and the blackness of the sable• tapestries became more terrifying. Those who stepped on the sable carpet heard a chime from the ebony clock that was more solemn• than any sound heard by those who were enjoying themselves in the other rooms.

THE MASKED BALL

Have you ever been to a fancy-dress party?
Who or what did you go as?
What was your costume like?
If you were going to a fancy-dress party now, what kind of costume would you like to wear?

18 The other apartments were densely crowded, and the heart of life beat in them feverishly•.

Glossary

- **back and forth:** backwards and forwards
- **feverishly:** in an excited or restless way
- **sable:** black
- **solemn:** grave; sad

The party went on, until soon the clock began to strike midnight. Then the music and the dancers and all other things stopped as before. But now twelve strokes• had to be sounded by the clock, and this gave the more thoughtful guests time to think. Before the last echoes of the last chime, many individuals in the crowd had noticed the presence of a masked figure that no one had seen before. The rumour of this new presence spread around in whispers. There was a murmur of disapproval from the whole company. Then this turned into a murmur of terror, of horror, and of disgust.

In an assembly of people like the ones I have described, someone of ordinary appearance would not have caused such feelings. Anything and everything was allowed that night, but the figure in question• had gone beyond even the prince's limits. There are chords• in the hearts of even the most badly behaved people that cannot be touched without causing emotion. There are some things about which it is impossible to joke. The whole company seemed now to feel that the costume and the behaviour of the stranger had no humour or good taste at all. The figure was tall and thin, and was shrouded• from head to foot in the clothes of the grave. The mask that hid the face resembled the face of a stiffened• corpse• so closely that it would have been difficult to tell the difference between the mask and a real face. While the guests did not approve of this, they might have tolerated it, but this actor had gone so far as to assume the appearance of the Red Death. His clothes were covered in blood – and his broad forehead and all the features of his face were sprinkled• with the scarlet horror.

- **chords:** (here) parts
- **corpse:** dead body
- **shrouded:** covered in the clothes of a dead person
- **sprinkled:** covered in small marks
- **stiffened:** rigid
- **strokes:** sounds of a bell or a clock to indicate a certain time
- **the figure in question:** the person we are discussing

When Prince Prospero saw this spectral figure walking among the dancers with a slow and solemn movement, at first he trembled either from terror or distaste but then his face reddened with rage.

'Who dares', he demanded hoarsely of the servants who stood near him. 'Who dares insult us with this blasphemous mockery? Stop him and unmask him, so that we may know whom we have to hang at sunrise from the tower!'

THE STRANGER

Who is the stranger?
What is strange about his behaviour?
What do you think he wants?
Why are the guests horrified by his appearance?
Why does he make Prince Prospero so angry?

Prince Prospero stood in the eastern or blue room as he spoke these words. They rang throughout the seven rooms loudly and clearly, for the prince was a bold, robust man, and the music had become hushed at the waving of his hand.

Glossary

- **blasphemous**: without respect; (speaking or acting) against God
- **distaste:** disgust
- **hang:** kill by hanging from a rope
- **hoarsely:** in a weak rough voice, as though he had lost his voice
- **hushed:** quiet
- **mockery:** making fun of someone or something in an unpleasant way
- **spectral:** like a ghost

The prince was standing in the blue room with a group of pale-faced servants by his side. At first, as he spoke, this group rushed in the direction of the intruder•, who at that moment was close by and who, with a deliberate step, moved closer to the prince. But everyone was so shocked by the actor that no one tried to stop him, and he moved close to the prince without being stopped. The great assembly, as if with one thought, moved back from the centres of the rooms to the walls. With the same solemn and measured• step which had distinguished him from the beginning, the figure made his way without interruption through the blue room into the purple, through the purple into the green, through the green into the orange, through this again into the white, and then into the violet room.
It was then, however, that Prince Prospero, mad with rage• and the shame of his own momentary cowardice•, rushed through the six rooms. No one followed him because of the terror that they all felt. The prince carried a dagger• and had approached rapidly to within three or four feet• of the figure, when the latter•, having reached the velvet room, turned suddenly and faced his pursuer•. There was a sharp cry – and the dagger dropped onto the sable carpet, upon which, instantly afterwards, Prince Prospero fell down dead.

Summoning• the wild courage of despair, a group of the guests ran into the black room and tried to stop the actor, whose tall figure stood motionless• in the shadow of the ebony clock. They gasped• in horror when they found that the shroud• and the corpse-like mask were not inhabited by any tangible form•.

Glossary

- **cowardice:** when you lack courage or bravery
- **dagger:** knife with a handle
- **feet:** one foot is approx 30 centimetres
- **gasped:** breathed loudly
- **held dominion:** ruled; commanded
- **intruder:** someone who has entered without permission
- **measured:** calculated
- **motionless:** without moving
- **pursuer:** person following

And now the presence of the Red Death was acknowledged. He had come like a thief in the night. And in the bloodstained halls of their celebration, one by one the partygoers dropped and died. And the life of the ebony clock went out with that of the last of the merry-makers. And the flames of the tripods went out, and darkness and decay and the Red Death held dominion• over all.

- **rage:** great anger
- **shroud:** cloth that covers a dead person
- **summoning:** gathering (energy/ courage etc.)
- **tangible form:** real person; someone or something that exists and can be touched
- **the latter:** the last person or thing mentioned

After Reading

The Three Stories

1 **Look at these three illustrations from the stories you have just read. In groups discuss the following questions.**

a) Which stories do they belong to?
b) Are they representative of the stories?
c) What are the similarities in the illustrations?
d) What are the differences?
e) Design a new cover for the book.

a

b

c

2 **Compare the three main characters of all three stories. What are the similarities? What are the differences? Discuss in pairs.**

Roderick Usher

The Painter

Prince Prospero

3 **What is the effect of the narrator in each story? Does he reflect the author's point of view? Is the narrator neutral or does he affect our interpretation of the story? Is the narrator reliable in these stories? Give reasons for your answers.**

Personal Response

1 **Work with a partner. What did you like the most about the story and what did you dislike the most?**

2 **Did this story remind you of any other stories you have read or films you have seen? Tell the rest of the class about them.**

3 **In which country do you think the story takes place? Give reasons for your answer.**

4 **When do you think the story takes place? Look for examples in the story to support your answer.**

5 **'He had come like a thief in the night.' Who is the author referring to? What does the author mean?**

6 **Is there anything in the story that you would have liked to change? Can you think of any way to improve the story?**

After Reading

Comprehension

1 Answer the following questions.

a) In the story, why was the disease called the 'Red Death'?
b) Why did the servants weld the bolts of the gates?
c) When was the disease at its worst?
d) How many friends did the prince take with him to the abbey?
e) What colour was the fourth room?
f) How were the guests dressed?
g) Which room were the guests afraid of and why?
h) What happened when the clock chimed?
i) At what time did the stranger appear?
j) What was the prince going to do to the stranger?
k) How did the prince die?
l) What happened to the guests at the ball?

2 Look again at the pictures illustrating this story. Write a short caption for each picture of one sentence or less.

3 In groups compare your captions. Choose one from each group for each picture.

4 Prince Prospero designed a suite of rooms. Which of the following colours did he use to decorate the rooms?

☐ green	☐ blue	☐ purple	☐ brown
☐ black	☐ yellow	☐ orange	☐ white
☐ red	☐ pink	☐ violet	☐ grey

5 Put these sentences from the story in the right order:

a) [1] The whole attack, progress and termination of the disease lasted half an hour.

b) [ ] It was an impressive scene, that masquerade.

c) [ ] And the life of the ebony clock went out with that of the last of the merry-makers.

d) [ ] There was no light of any kind from lamps or candles inside the rooms.

e) [ ] The rumour of this new presence spread around in whispers.

f) [ ] The prince was standing in the blue room with a group of pale-faced servants by his side.

g) [ ] But when the echoes of the chimes had stopped, laughter immediately spread through the group.

h) [ ] The prince had provided everything that would give pleasure.

6 Find words in the story that match the meanings below:

a) A type of party
b) A set of rooms
c) A kind of knife
d) A sound made by a clock
e) The glass in a window
f) People who play in an orchestra

7 Use your imagination to complete this invitation to Prince Prospero's party. Include the following information:

- Time
- Date
- Place
- Dress code
- Entertainment

Prince Prospero has great pleasure in inviting you to a ...

After Reading

Characters

1 Imagine you are a reporter who is going to interview Prince Prospero, the narrator and the uninvited stranger. Prepare three questions for each of them. Next, work with two or three other students. Read your questions out to the group.

2 Work with a partner to write up your interview with one of the story's three characters. Act out your interview to the rest of the class.

3 Who is the 'actor' who appears at the Prince's party? Describe him. Why are the partygoers horrified by him?

4 How does Prince Prospero's reaction to the events in his country reveal his character?

5 Does Poe approve of Prince Prospero and his actions? Discuss in pairs.

6 Prince Prospero is writing a journal. Some of his words have faded from the parchment. Use words from the story to complete his entry.

We have now been here in the .... for about .... or .... months. We have plenty of .... and tomorrow I will .... my friends to a .... ball. I will, of course, hold this in the .... of .... rooms that I have personally designed. The .... are built in an .... way and each one is decorated in a different .... My favourite room is the black room, which is on the .... side. Its colour is .... and its walls are covered in velvet .... of the same colour. The windows here are a deep .... colour. The effect this creates is .... in the extreme. I'm sure no one will be .... enough to set .... inside this room. I think I'm going to have a lot of fun.

7 Work with a partner to write another entry from Prince Prospero's journal. Read this entry to the class.

After Reading

Plot and Theme

1 Work with two or three other students and discuss the following statements. Are any of these the message of the story?

a) Life is short so enjoy it while you can.
b) You can escape many things but not death.
c) We cannot help everyone so we must look after ourselves.
d) In difficult times, we should always be positive.

2 What do you think is the significance of the following:

a) The seven rooms? Think about what other things come in groups of seven.
b) The gigantic ebony clock? Think about how the clock is described.
c) The prince's name? What do you think it means?
d) The words 'masque', 'mask' and 'masquerade'? Use your dictionary to help you understand these words.

3 If you have read *The Fall of the House of Usher*, did you notice any similarities between that story and this one? Can you match the events from *The Fall of the House of Usher* with the following phrases from *The Masque of the Red Death*?

a) ☐ Lady Madeline was suffering from a disease that her doctors could not cure.

b) ☐ Roderick Usher had a strange collection of books.

c) ☐ Usher and his sister fall down dead on the ground.

d) ☐ Usher and the narrator seal the lid of Lady Madeline's coffin and lock the vault's iron door.

e) ☐ Usher invites the narrator to stay at his house and keep him company.

1 '... the prince's love of bizarre things ...'
2 '... he called into his presence a thousand healthy and cheerful friends ...'
3 'No pestilence had ever been so fatal, or so terrible.'
4 'This wall had iron gates. The servants, using furnaces and hammers, welded the bolts of the gates.'
5 '... instantly afterwards, Prince Prospero fell down dead ...'

4 Work with your partner and try to find examples of links between the two stories. Share these with the rest of the class.

5 Poe's Red Death resembles a real disease that was present in Europe in the Middle Ages: the Bubonic Plague or Black Death. What contagious diseases are still a problem in today's world? What is being done to stop them?

6 Childhood illnesses and infections are rapidly disappearing in many countries due to advances in medicine and inoculation campaigns. What illnesses of this kind do you know about, and have you ever suffered from one? How long did it last and what were the symptoms? What helped you recover?

After Reading

Test

1 Read the description of Prince Prospero and choose the most suitable word for each space.

A terrible plague was devastating the country and half the population had **(a)** .... died. Prince Prospero, **(b)** .... was a wise man, decided to escape to the safety of an isolated abbey with a thousand of his healthy friends. He locked **(c)** .... and his friends into the abbey and he locked the world and the plague out. He left his people to their terrible fate.

After five or six months of isolation, the Prince decided to entertain his friends with a magnificent masked ball. The ball **(d)** .... in a suite of seven rooms and each room was decorated in a different colour. The seventh room was decorated in black and it had blood red windows, which cast ghastly shadows **(e)** .... the room and the guests. Not many people had the courage to enter this room.

When the clock struck midnight, some of the guests noticed a masked figure that they **(f)** .... before. To the horror and disgust of the assembled guests, the masked figure had dressed **(g)** .... a victim of the Red Death.

At first Prince Prospero was afraid but then his fear turned to anger. Who dares to mock us? He cried. He shall be hung **(h)** .... dawn. The masked corpse moved towards the prince and the guests moved back. The masked figure moved slowly towards the black room and the Prince followed. When he reached the black room, he turned and faced the Prince. Prince Prospero let out a cry and fell down dead.

	1	2	3	4
a)	**1** almost	**2** already	**3** yet	**4** although
b)	**1** who	**2** that	**3** whose	**4** which
c)	**1** herself	**2** his own	**3** him	**4** himself
d)	**1** was holding	**2** were held	**3** was held	**4** held
e)	**1** across	**2** under	**3** behind	**4** out of
f)	**1** didn't see	**2** hadn't seen	**3** haven't seen	**4** weren't seen
g)	**1** as	**2** of	**3** for	**4** from
h)	**1** for	**2** in	**3** on	**4** at

2 Imagine that you were the only guest at the masked ball to survive. Write a letter to a friend in another country and tell him/her all about the ball.

What did you wear?
How were the rooms decorated?
How did you feel about the black room?
Did you go in there?
What happened at the ball?
How did you escape?
Do you approve of what Prince Prospero did?

3 With a partner look at the picture on page 94. Ask and answer questions about it.

How do the people in the picture feel?

They are very frightened.

4 Read the questions and tick (✓) the most suitable answers.

a) How could you tell that someone had the Red Death?
1 ☐ The victims had a red mark on their noses.
2 ☐ They had red marks on their bodies and on their faces.
3 ☐ They had red marks on their feet.
4 ☐ Their bodies were red.

b) What did Prince Prospero and his friends eat inside the abbey?
1 ☐ Food was brought to them daily.
2 ☐ They ate in restaurants in the neighbourhood.
3 ☐ They didn't eat.
4 ☐ They ate the supplies already inside the abbey.

c) The seven rooms, in which the masked ball were held, were arranged so that … .
1 ☐ all the rooms could be clearly seen.
2 ☐ you could only see the room you were in.
3 ☐ you could see into the next room.
4 ☐ you could see into each of the seven rooms.

d) Why did the musicians stop playing when the gigantic ebony clock struck the hour?
1 ☐ They were tired and needed a break every hour.
2 ☐ They liked the sound that the clock made.
3 ☐ The guests wanted to know what time it was.
4 ☐ They were very strongly affected by the chimes of the clock.

e) When did the guests start to notice the figure dressed as the Red Death?
1 ☐ After the death of Prince Prospero.
2 ☐ When the clock chimed at midnight.
3 ☐ When one of the guests screamed.
4 ☐ When Prince Prospero told them to unmask the terrible figure.